MOG'S
Christmas

MOG'S
Christmas

written and illustrated by

Judith Kerr

HarperCollins *Children's Books*

For my friend
Mrs Cleghorn

Other books by Judith Kerr include:

Mog the Forgetful Cat

Mog and the Baby

Mog in the Dark

Mog's Amazing Birthday Caper

Mog and Bunny

Mog and Barnaby

Mog on Fox Night

Mog and the Granny

Mog and the Vee Ee Tee

Mog's Bad Thing

Goodbye Mog

Birdie Halleluyah!

The Tiger Who Came to Tea

The Other Goose

Twinkles, Arthur and Puss

First published in hardback in Great Britain by William Collins Sons & Co Ltd in 1976. First published in paperback in 1978.
This edition published by HarperCollins Children's Books in 2004

10 9 8 7

ISBN-13: 978-0-00-717135-4

Visit our website at. www.harpercollins.co.uk

Printed and bound by Printing Express, Hong Kong

One day Mog woke up
and nothing was right in her house.

Everybody was busy.
Debbie was busy.

Nicky was busy.

Mr and Mrs Thomas
were busy.

And there were too many
people in the house.

There was a jolly uncle

...and two aunts
on tippy-toe.

Mog thought, "I don't like it here."
She went and sat outside on the window-sill.
There was nothing to do and no one to play
with, so after a while she went back to sleep.

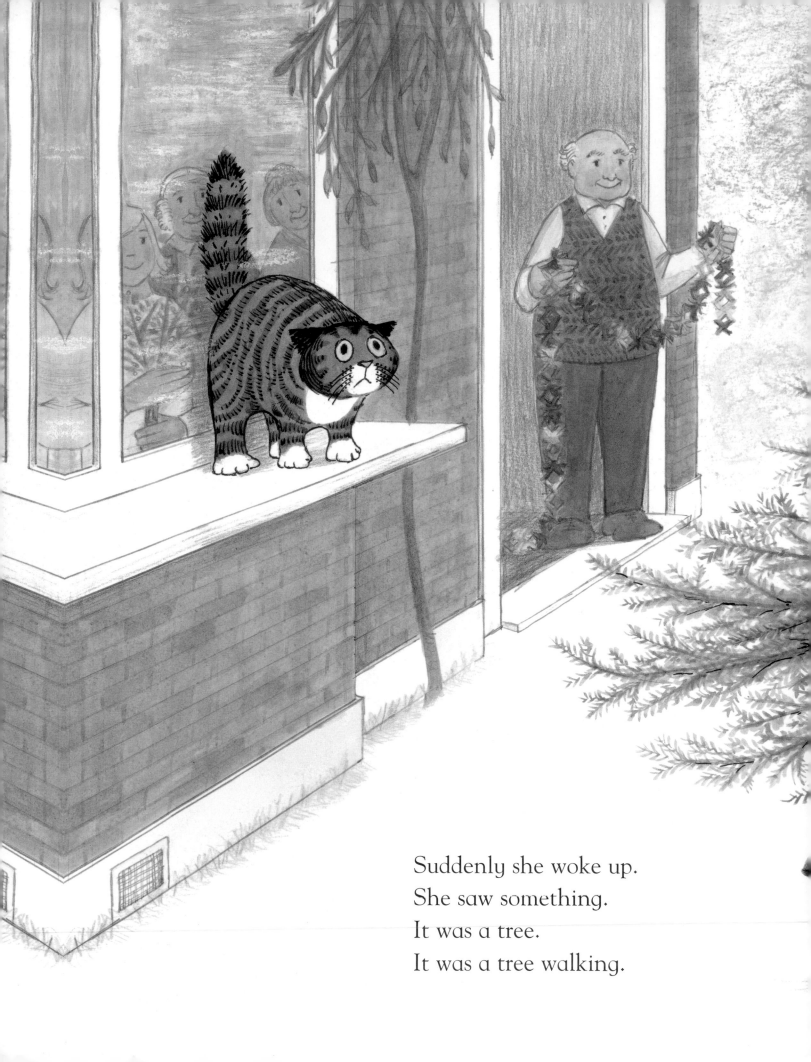

Suddenly she woke up.
She saw something.
It was a tree.
It was a tree walking.

Mog thought, "Trees don't walk.
Trees should stay in one place.
Once trees start walking about
anything might happen."
She ran up the side of the
house in case the tree should
come and get her.
"Come down," shouted the tree.
"Come down, Mog!"
"First it walks," thought Mog,
"and now it's shouting at me.
I do not like that tree at all."
And she ran right up to the roof.

The tree went on shouting for a while.
Then it went into the house.
Mog stayed on the roof.
Some white things fell out of the sky.
Some fell on the roof and some fell
on Mog.
They were very cold.

At supper time
Mog was still on the roof.
"She must have her supper,"
said Debbie. "Mog always
has her supper."
Mrs Thomas gave Mog her supper.
But still Mog did not come down.

In the morning Mog did not come down either.
She had found a nice tall place, and she
was asleep.
She was having a lovely dream.

Mog dreamed that she was sitting on a cloud.
Some white things were falling out of the sky.
Mog tried to catch them. She was very happy.
But suddenly the cloud began to melt...

Inside the house everyone was sad
because Mog would not come down.
They were too sad to eat their breakfast.

Even the jolly uncle was sad,
and one of the aunts cried.

Mog had to have a bath.
But then...

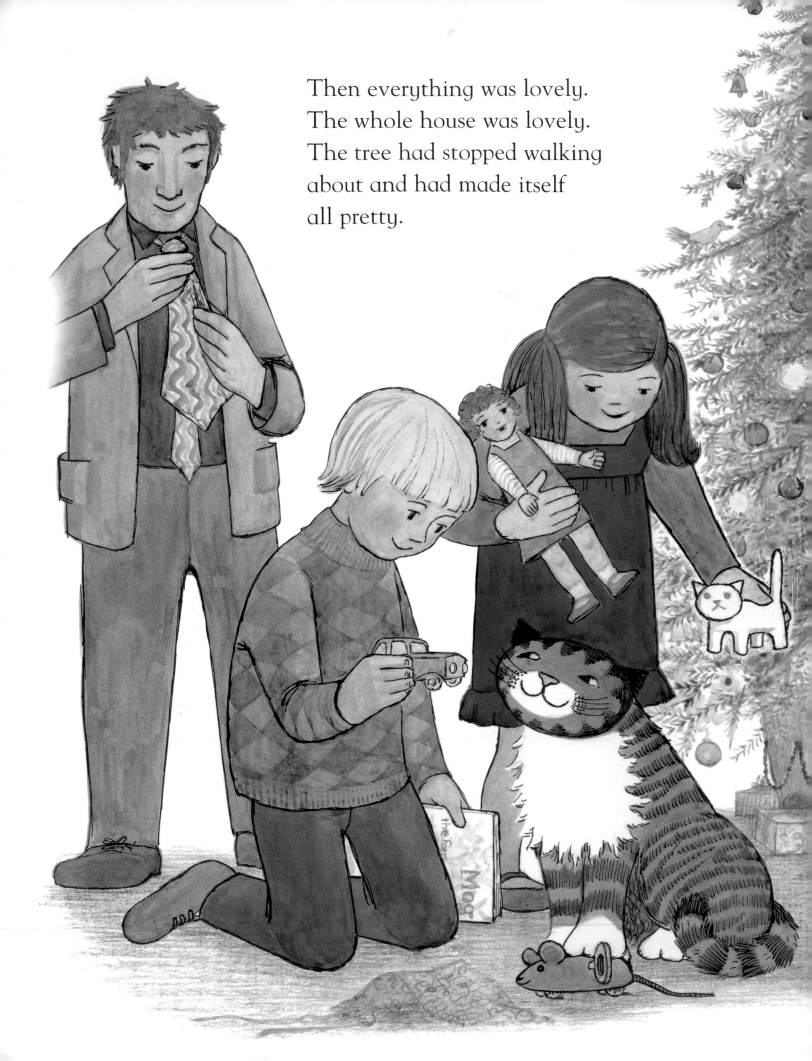

Then everything was lovely.
The whole house was lovely.
The tree had stopped walking
about and had made itself
all pretty.

And Mog had three boiled eggs and
some turkey and a present to unwrap.

"Happy Christmas, Mog," said Debbie.